Dedicated with thanks to Chris Chapman,
who first introduced me to the writings of Etty Hillesum
—A. B.

For Katie, Benny, George, & Maggie
—D. L.

Anne Booth was inspired to write this book by the words of Etty Hillesum,

a Jewish woman and victim of the Holocaust who wrote:

"Give your sorrow all the space and shelter in yourself that is its due,

for if everyone bears grief honestly and courageously, the sorrow that now fills the world will abate.

But if you do instead reserve most of the space inside you for hatred and thoughts of revenge—from which new sor-

rows will be born for others—then sorrow will never cease in this world.

And if you have given sorrow the space it demands, then you may truly say: life is beautiful and so rich."

Esther "Etty" Hillesum (15 Jan. 1914–30 Nov. 1943)

Published by
PEACHTREE PUBLISHING COMPANY INC.
1700 Chattahoochee Avenue
Atlanta, Georgia 30318-2112
www.peachtree-online.com

Text © 2021 by Anne Booth
Illustrations © 2021 by David Litchfield

First published in the United Kingdom in 2021 by Templar Books, an imprint of Bonnier Books UK, The Plaza, 535 King's Road, London, SW10 0SZ
First United States version published in 2021 by Peachtree Publishing Company Inc.

The illustrations were created with watercolor, acrylic, pen, ink, and Adobe Photoshop.

Printed in May 2021 in China
10 9 8 7 6 5 4 3 2 1
First Edition

ISBN 978-1-68263-339-7

Cataloging-in-Publication Data is available from the Library of Congress

a Shelter for Sadness

ANNE BOOTH & DAVID LITCHFIELD

PEACHTREE

ATLANTA

Sadness has come to live with me,
and I am building it a shelter.

I am building a shelter
for my sadness
and welcoming it inside.

I am giving it
a space to sit

or lie down.

To curl up very,
very small,

or be as **big** as it can be.

To run around

or stand still.

To be **very, very noisy,**

or very, very quiet.

Or anything in between.

In this shelter, my sadness can turn to the wall

or look out through the window . . .

in the middle of the night or in the day.

The windows will open to let sounds in,

or close to keep them out.

The shelter I build

for my sadness

will have light from the sun,

or from the moon and stars.

But the windows will have curtains

that my sadness can draw when it wants to.

And light, if it wants,

from candles or lamps.

Lots and lots of light,

or no light at all.

My sadness can sit in darkness if it wants to.

Whatever it feels like.

Because this is the shelter for my sadness,

and it has a right to be there.

And I will make my shelter strong, so that in winter

my sadness will be safe against the storms.

But I will give it a little garden too,

so that in spring, birds will come and build their nests

and green shoots will peek through the dark earth.

In summer, roses will bloom,
and their scent will steal in under the door.
And my sadness can open the windows
and breath in and smell them.

If it wants to.

In autumn, my sadness
can look out at the trees and cry
when the leaves turn red and orange
and fall to the ground.

Or it can go out and run through the leaves
and hear the sounds they make.

It can build bonfires and dance around them,

or sit quietly and watch the flames.

Anything it needs to.

Sometimes I will visit my sadness
in its shelter every day.

Every hour if needed.

Sometimes we will run

into each other's arms and hug and cry,

and talk . . .

and sometimes just sit next to each other

saying nothing.

Sometimes I will be too busy to visit my sadness for a while.

But that's okay too.

I have built a shelter for my sadness

and it is safe inside, and nobody will hurt it.

I can visit whenever I need to.
Whenever it calls to me.

And whenever my sadness wants,
it can come out of its shelter
and hold my hand.

And we will look out at the world
and discover how beautiful it is.
Together.